D1156820

Take Your Pet to the Vet

Adapted by Sara Miller
Based on the episode written by Ford Riley
Based on the series created by Chris Nee
Illustrated by Character Building Studio and the Disney Storybook Art Team

ABDOPUBLISHING.COM

Reinforced library bound edition published in 2019 by Spotlight, a division of ABDO, PO Box 398166, Minneapolis, Minnesota 55439. Spotlight produces high-quality reinforced library bound editions for schools and libraries. Published by agreement with Disney Press, an imprint of Disney Book Group.

Printed in the United States of America, North Mankato, Minnesota.
042018   092018

D𝒾𝑠𝑛𝑒𝓎 PRESS
New York • Los Angeles

THIS BOOK CONTAINS
RECYCLED MATERIALS

Library of Congress Control Number: 2017961159

Publisher's Cataloging in Publication Data

Names: Miller, Sara, author. | Riley, Ford, author. | Character Building Studio; Disney Storybook Art Team, illustrators.
Title: Doc McStuffins: Take your pet to the vet / by Sara Miller and Ford Riley; illustrated by Character Building Studio and Disney Storybook Art Team.
Description: Minneapolis, MN : Spotlight, 2019 | Series: World of reading level 1
Summary: Doc brings home her class pet, Coleslaw the hamster, for the weekend. After a day of playing with the toys, Coleslaw isn't acting like herself. Doc decides to take her to the vet.
Identifiers: ISBN 9781532141881 (lib. bdg.)
Subjects: LCSH: Doc McStuffins (Television program)--Juvenile fiction. | Hamsters as pets--Juvenile fiction. | Veterinarians--Juvenile fiction. | Common cold--Juvenile fiction. | Readers (Primary)--Juvenile fiction.
Classification: DDC [E]--dc23

Spotlight
A Division of ABDO
abdopublishing.com

Doc is bringing home a new pet today!
She will be here soon.
The toys can't wait to meet the new pet.

Doc and Chilly are home from school.
They have a cute little hamster!

"Meet my good friend," Chilly says.
"Her name is Coleslaw."

Doc puts the cage down.
The toys say hi to Coleslaw.

Coleslaw loves to run on her wheel.
She runs around and around.

Doc takes Coleslaw out of her cage.
She puts Coleslaw into her hamster ball.

Coleslaw loves to run and play.
Look at her go!

Coleslaw has had a long day.
It is time for bed.

Chilly wants to sleep next to his friend.
"Good night, Coleslaw," Chilly says.

Chilly wakes up the next day.
He wants to play with Coleslaw.

But Coleslaw does not want
to run or play.
Is Coleslaw okay?

Chilly rushes to Doc's clinic.
"Doc, you have to help!" he says.

Doc wants to help.

But Coleslaw needs a doctor for pets.

She needs a vet.

Mom and Doc take Coleslaw to the vet.
There are a lot of pets here today.

They wait for their turn to see the vet.
Chilly hopes Coleslaw will be okay.

Soon the vet is ready to see Coleslaw.
The vet's name is Dr. Reese.
Dr. Reese checks Coleslaw's heartbeat.
She checks Coleslaw's eyes and ears.

Ti-choo! Coleslaw sneezes.
Dr. Reese has a diagnosis.

Coleslaw has a cold!

Chilly feels bad.

"I am a snowman. I am cold," he says.

"I gave Coleslaw a cold!"

"Don't worry, Chilly," says Doc.

"You are not a real snowman."

Chilly feels better.

Dr. Reese says Coleslaw will be better soon. She just needs to rest. "That's great!" says Doc.

Later that night, Doc checks
on her pet.

"I gave Coleslaw food and water,"
says Chilly. "I hope she will be okay."

"Coleslaw just needs to rest," says Doc. "And so do we."

"Good night, Coleslaw,"
says Chilly. "Feel better soon."

Chilly wakes up the next morning.
Coleslaw is all better!

30

Coleslaw wants to run and play.
Look at her go!

Coleslaw is one happy hamster.
And Chilly is one happy snowman.